TOOGA

THE STORY OF A POLAR BEAR

SHIRLEY WOODS

ILLUSTRATED BY MURIEL WOOD

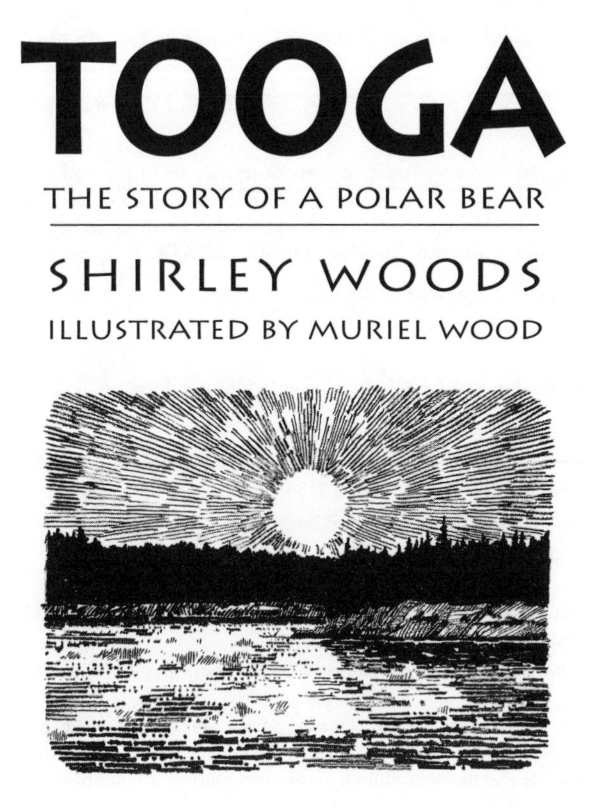

Fitzhenry & Whiteside

Published in Canada by Fitzhenry & Whiteside, 195 Allstate Parkway, Markham, Ontario L3R 4T8

Published in the United States by Fitzhenry & Whiteside, 121 Harvard Avenue, Suite 2, Allston, Massachusetts 02134

www.fitzhenry.ca godwit@fitzhenry.ca.

10 9 8 7 6 5 4 3 2 1

Library and Archives Canada Cataloguing in Publication Data

Woods, Shirley E.

Tooga : the story of a polar bear / Shirley Woods ; illustrations by Muriel Wood.

ISBN 1-55041-898-X (bound).—ISBN 1-55041-900-5 (pbk.)

1. Polar bear—Juvenile fiction. I. Wood, Muriel II. Title.

PS8595.O652T65 2004 jC813'.54 C2004-903690-4

U.S. Publisher Cataloging-in-Publication Data (Library of Congress Standards)

Woods, Shirley.
Tooga : the story of a polar bear / Shirley Woods ; illustrations by Muriel Wood. –1st ed.
[96] p. : ill. ; cm.
Summary: On the coast of northern Labrador, a polar bear mother teaches her young how to hunt and survive. Just when the young male is ready to hunt for himself, he becomes trapped on an ice floe that drifts hundreds of miles south and into unfamiliar territory.
ISBN 1-55041-898-X
ISBN 1-55041-900-5 (pbk.)
1. Polar bear — Fiction — Juvenile literature. 2. Labrador (N.L.) — Juvenile fiction.
I. Wood, Muriel. I. Title.
[Fic] dc22 PZ7.W6637To 2004

Fitzhenry & Whiteside acknowledges with thanks the Canada Council for the Arts, the Government of Canada through the Book Publishing Industry Development Program (BPIDP), and the Ontario Arts Council for their support of our publishing program.

Design by Blair Kerrigan/Glyphics
Printed in Canada

For Rosie and Jess

Author's Acknowledgements
Although this book is a novel, I have tried to ensure that the story is true to nature. In the course of my research I received help from many people, and I would particularly like to thank:

Ian Stirling, world authority on polar bears and senior research scientist for the Canadian Wildlife Service, who took the time to answer a variety of perplexing questions and whose book *Polar Bears* (University of Michigan Press, Ann Arbor, 1998), was my definitive reference source.

Bruce Turner, head of the Canadian Wildlife Service in Newfoundland and Labrador, who provided invaluable assistance by directing me to people with special knowledge of the polar bears on the coast of Labrador.

Harry Martin, provincial wildlife officer and longtime resident of Cartwright, Labrador, was immensely helpful in giving detailed information concerning polar bears, the weather, and ice conditions in the Sandwich Bay area.

Toby Anderson of Nain, Labrador provided firsthand knowledge of the geography, flora and fauna in Saglek Bay as well as the ice conditions along the northern coast of Labrador.

And finally I must thank Charlie White of St. John's, with whom I spent a week on the Eagle River, for sharing some of his personal encounters with bears and for giving me a copy of Captain Cartwright's Labrador journal.

NUNAVUT
GREENLAND
Hudson Bay
Labrador Sea
Saglek Bay
Tooga's Journey
Makkovik
LABRADOR
Cartwright
White Bear R.
Eagle R.
QUEBEC
NEWFOUNDLAND
St. John's
Atlantic Ocean
Boston
N
0
500 km
0
300 mi

Chapter One

THE MOTHER BEAR

A blizzard swept the coast of northern Labrador on the tenth of November. By noon it was nearly dark. Out on the sea ice, a white bear plodded through the blowing snow. Despite the failing light, she knew exactly where she was going. Ursa was returning to her birthplace, Saglek Bay, to have her cubs.

•

Early that spring Ursa had met a male polar bear on the ice farther up the coast. The two bears had mated and traveled together for more than a week. When they parted, Ursa had stayed out on the sea ice hunting seals.

Hunting was good in the spring. Adult seals and

their fat young pups were plentiful on the pack ice, and they could also be found close to shore on the fast ice — the ice that formed each fall and was attached (or fast) to the land.

Though smaller than a male bear, Ursa was a skilled hunter. What she lacked in size she made up for in cunning. By the end of June, when the ice broke up and she was forced to return to land, she had doubled her weight on a rich diet of seal meat and blubber.

Life on shore was much harder for her than on the ice floes. Summer temperatures were often uncomfortably hot, and food was scarce. Seals, her favorite prey, were now swimming freely in the ocean. Though a strong swimmer, she couldn't catch seals in the open sea.

For the rest of the summer Ursa ate whatever she could find, including seaweed, tundra grass, berries, and carrion washed up on the beach. She was always hungry, and without enough food she was becoming thinner. Being an expectant mother, she couldn't afford to lose weight. From the time she entered her natal den in the autumn until the following spring, she would have nothing to eat. Without a reserve of fat to draw upon, she and her cubs wouldn't survive the winter.

As soon as the sea froze in October, Ursa returned to the offshore floes. Autumn was a more difficult time to catch seals. By then the seal pups could take care of themselves, and the adult seals were always wary. Ursa knew that her hunting prospects were poor, but she craved the taste of blubber.

During the two days that it took her to walk to the edge of the pack ice, she didn't encounter a seal. On the third day her luck changed. She was climbing a low ridge when she smelled a delicious odor. Following her nose, she discovered a seal sunbathing on the ice near its breathing hole. Ursa stalked the seal so quietly that, when she made her final rush, it couldn't escape.

After gorging on the seal's skin and blubber, Ursa fell asleep. While she slept, a little white fox appeared from behind a snowdrift. Kwa, the arctic fox, had been following Ursa, waiting for her to make a kill. With one eye on the sleeping bear, Kwa tiptoed over to the carcass and began tearing pieces of meat from it.

Ursa had known that she was being followed,

having noticed Kwa's dainty footprints earlier in the day. The fox was neither a friend nor an enemy. So long as he kept his distance and didn't interfere with her, she would let him have the leftovers from her kills.

The fox and the polar bear roamed the pack ice together for several weeks. During this short period, Ursa caught enough seals to replace some of the fat she had lost. Kwa, trailing behind her, made sure that he got his share of the bounty.

•

On the morning of the ninth of November — the day before the big storm — Ursa experienced an odd sensation. She was standing on her hind legs, scanning the ice floe, when she felt the cubs stir in her belly. Up to that moment, her main concern had been to feed herself. Now a deep-seated instinct told her to stop hunting and return to land.

That same day she started for shore, picking her way through the frozen slush and jumbled blocks of ice. When the blizzard struck the next day, she kept on going. Around midnight, she stopped in the lee of a snow ridge to rest. While she slept, the sky cleared and the storm moved out to sea.

When she woke, the morning sun was a yellow streak on the horizon. Ursa stretched and shook the snow from her coat. Sniffing the breeze, she looked around. In the distance she could see the hills framing Saglek Bay. Satisfied that she was still headed in the right direction, she continued on her journey.

Presently she came to a spot where the water had welled through the ice, creating a small lake. The bear checked to see if there were any seals — or even a stranded beluga whale — in the shallow water. When she saw nothing, she skirted the lake and resumed her trek.

As she progressed, the wintry landscape became more open. Soon she noticed another change. The surface felt smoother underfoot; and where the snow had blown away, it was more slippery — signs that she had reached the new ice close to land.

Ursa was within a few hundred paces of the shore when she found her way blocked by a strip of open water. The winds and the force of the tide had split the ice, opening a channel shaped like the blade of a knife. The bear paused at the edge of the ice to consider the situation.

Swinging her long neck from side to side, she

looked up and down the channel. Either way it would be a long walk around the opening. In front of her the channel was no wider than a good-sized stream. Ursa slipped into the frigid water and, with a few strokes of her broad front paws, paddled to the other side.

•

The white fox had followed the bear all the way to Saglek Bay. But he refused to follow her when she swam to shore. Lemmings, the hamster-like rodents that arctic foxes depend upon for food, were very scarce that year. Kwa feared that if he spent the winter on land, he would starve. With a flick of his sausage-shaped tail, the little fox turned and headed back to the floes.

•

When Ursa reached the other side of the channel, she gripped the ice with her black claws and hauled herself out of the sea. Then, bracing her legs, she shook herself so violently that water flew in every direction.

Cold water and sub-zero temperatures didn't bother her. Like all polar bears she was well insulated against the cold with a thick layer of blubber and two layers of fur. The outer layer of her fur was coarse and straight. Beneath these long guard hairs, a dense layer of wooly underfur trapped the heat.

After shaking the water from her coat, Ursa used her tongue to groom her fur until it was smooth. In the sunlight the color of her coat wasn't pure white but tinged with yellow, like old ivory. When she had finished grooming herself, she left the beach and went inland.

As she walked along, she stopped frequently to study her surroundings. She was searching for a place to have her cubs. For safety, the birthing den had to be far enough inland so that it wouldn't be noticed. But it also had to be close enough to the bay so that it wouldn't be too long a walk for her cubs in the spring.

When Ursa was satisfied that she was the proper distance from the water, she looked around for a snowdrift on the side of a slope. There were lots of drifts to choose from. Ursa wanted a drift that faced south, so the prevailing north wind would pile snow on the den all winter, and the sun would warm it in the spring. Not only must it face south but the snow had to be firm enough to scoop out a den.

The bear tested several drifts with a swipe of her paw until she found one where the snow was just right. Carefully she dug into the drift and hollowed out a cavity the size and shape of a large bathtub. To retain the heat, she made sure her birthing chamber was raised above the narrow entrance tunnel. As a finishing touch, she scraped a small hole with her claws in the snow ceiling for ventilation.

That night she moved into the den. The heat of her body, combined with the insulation of the snow, soon raised the inside temperature. The den was snug and warm, but the babies within her were so active that it was hard to find a comfortable resting position.

Although polar bears don't hibernate in winter, as the days passed Ursa's heartbeat slowed and she dozed for long periods while she waited for her babies to be born.

Chapter Two

A BEAR IS BORN

On the fifth of December a heavy snowfall covered the slope, sealing the entrance to Ursa's den. The only sign left of the bear's presence was a small hole in the drift. An intruder would have had to look closely to see that Ursa's breath had melted the snow that rimmed the vent, and that she was inside.

Ursa's two cubs were born soon after the moon rose. That night, as if to greet them, the northern lights put on a spectacular display. It began with a shimmering green glow on the horizon and ended with a cluster of red streamers that soared like fireworks above the den before fading into the darkness.

As each cub was born, Ursa cleaned it with her tongue and then gently placed it on her stomach close to a nipple. Within minutes both cubs were sucking lustily, nestled in their mother's warm fur. The larger of the two cubs was a male. His name was Tooga. His sister's name was Apoon.

The cubs were about the size of half-grown kittens — tiny compared to their mother. At birth they were covered with fine white fur. Although their eyes and ears were sealed and they could barely move, they had little claws. These they used like combs to part their mother's fur when searching for a nipple.

For the first weeks Ursa's babies required constant care. As well as frequent feedings, she also had to keep a close eye on them. If a cub slipped unnoticed onto the snow floor, it could die of the cold. Even when Ursa slept, she had to take care lest she roll on them.

In early January, when the cubs were a month old, they opened their eyes. At about the same time, they began to crawl. By now their fur was thick enough so that the cold floor was no longer a danger. As they became stronger, they tried to crawl over their mother. This was difficult, as neither could grip onto her long and glassy fur.

Tooga, after many attempts, finally managed to climb up his mother's side. When he started down the other side, however, he lost his grip and slid to the floor with a thump. As soon as he got over his fright, he climbed back up and did it again. Apoon followed close behind. For the next few weeks, sliding down their mother was their favorite pastime.

Tooga and Apoon took their first shaky steps at the beginning of February. Within a few weeks they could walk steadily and could even stand — briefly — on their hind legs. From walking they quickly graduated to running. This new skill led to games of chase around their long-suffering mother.

During the February storms, snow often blocked the vent. When this happened, Ursa would scrape the snow away from the inside to enlarge the opening. Her cubs, who learned by watching their mother, tried to copy her. But they couldn't reach the ceiling.

Instead, Tooga and Apoon dug into the walls. Working together, they managed to scoop out a narrow tunnel that eventually curved from one end of the den to the other. The moment it was finished, the cubs used it for games of chase and hide-and-seek.

•

By the first of March, there was some warmth in the sun. The coldest and darkest months had passed. Inside the den, the spot of sunlight coming through the vent took longer to cross the floor each day.

One morning, the cubs were surprised to see their mother digging into the wall of the den. They had often seen her scrape snow from the ceiling, but she had never touched the walls before. Their mother worked steadily, and soon only her haunches were visible in the tunnel. As the cubs watched, she suddenly disappeared. All that remained was a circle of light.

Tooga and Apoon were terrified and fled to a corner of the den.

A few minutes later their mother's head reappeared at the exit hole. She called the cubs, but they were too frightened to move. After a moment she climbed back into the den to comfort them. When they'd been fed, she tried again to get them to follow her outside.

Tooga, with much coaxing, went as far as the end of the tunnel. Gingerly, he poked his nose out the exit hole. The air was cold and smelled quite different from the den. Pushing his head out farther he looked around, but the sunlight on the snow was so bright that it made his eyes smart. The little bear backed down the hole to the familiar darkness of the den.

Their mother returned in less than an hour to spend the night with them. The next morning she went outside again. Once more she tried to persuade the cubs to come with her. This time Apoon joined Tooga at the exit hole, but neither cub would step outside. They were quite content, however, to watch their mother walk around on the snow nearby.

The cubs were now three months of age. With their soft wooly coats, snub noses, and black button eyes, they looked like white teddy bears. Since birth, they had increased their weight more than tenfold on the high-fat diet of their mother's milk.

•

The cubs finally went outside with their mother on the third morning. Ursa stayed close to them, and all went well until a raven flew by. When the raven spied the bear family, it swooped over and uttered a loud *Krok!* At the sound of the bird's harsh call, Tooga and Apoon bolted into the den.

Ursa had to comfort and feed her babies before they would come out again. To be on the safe side, the cubs checked the sky for unwelcome visitors. By then the raven — who was harmless — had flown away. Once they were satisfied the sky was clear, they resumed their play outside, wrestling and tumbling down the slope.

The cubs didn't know it, but this brief outing marked a turning point in their lives. For the next two weeks they spent their nights in the den, with longer periods outside each day. Their mother was preparing them for their long trek on the sea ice.

Tooga and his sister soon became accustomed to the dazzling sunlight and colder temperatures outside. Nor was the wind a problem after the stillness of the den, even though it ruffled their fur and sometimes made their noses tingle. Being used to the hard-packed floor of the den, however, they found it very tiring to walk in the soft snow.

To strengthen their legs, their mother took them for short walks every day. Ursa led, with Tooga and Apoon following close behind her. Some days Ursa would set off in one direction and sometimes in another, but the route was always a circle that ended up back at the den.

Ursa kept a close watch on her babies. When they

encountered heavy snow, she would stop to give them a rest. While they rested, she would comfort them with nose touches, and groom them with her tongue. On these short walks she didn't nurse the cubs. But she fed them outside every day in a snow pit she had dug to shelter them from the wind.

•

One day in mid-March, as soon as Tooga and Apoon emerged from the den, their mother took them on a walk. This was unusual, as the cubs' routine outside normally began with a period of play. Even stranger, this morning their mother didn't lead them in a circle. Instead, she headed toward the bay.

The journey to the sea ice had begun.

CHAPTER THREE

LEAVING THE DEN

A white gyrfalcon soared over the granite hills of Saglek Bay. This bird — the largest of all falcons — could see the snow-covered rocks below as clearly as a human looking through binoculars. When the falcon reached the edge of the hills without finding any prey, he flew on over the treeless tundra.

The gyrfalcon rode the wind, scanning the lowland that bordered the frozen bay. In the distance, he saw a polar bear and two cubs wending their way though a patch of willow bushes. The falcon wasn't interested in the bears.

But he had often found ptarmigan — the northern cousins of the ruffed grouse — among the willows. Sideslipping into the wind, the falcon flew with rapid wing beats over to check the willows. When he was directly above the bears, he saw the mother bear suddenly stop. At the same instant, a flock of ptarmigan erupted from the snow at her feet and flew off with a rush.

The gyrfalcon tipped his body forward, half-folded his long pointed wings, and dove at the departing ptarmigan. As he dropped, gaining speed every second, the falcon kept his eyes focused on a single bird at the rear of the flock.

•

Once again Tooga bumped into his mother's hind leg. He was always bumping into her, for she often stopped without warning. But this time was different — his mother had nearly stepped on some white birds nestled in the snow.

When the ptarmigan flushed from under his mother's nose, it gave him a fright. Tooga watched them speed away like arrows, cackling, *Go beck, go beck!* They hadn't flown far before a white falcon plummeted from the sky and struck one of them a terrific blow. The ptarmigan tumbled to the ground in a puff of feathers, closely followed by the falcon.

While Tooga and Apoon watched the ptarmigan, their mother sniffed the wind. For the first time on their journey, she smelled another polar bear. Her hackles rose when she recognized the scent. It was Panak, a large male who was so bad-tempered that he attacked smaller bears and even cubs.

Panak was somewhere out on the ice, not far away. Fortunately Ursa and the cubs were downwind of him, so he couldn't smell them. But the mother bear knew that her family was still in danger. They must leave the area at once, before Panak saw them.

Ursa nudged the cubs and snorted for them to move on. Keeping to the snowy shoreline, she led them deeper into the bay. She was taking them to a place where there were fewer seals and less risk of encountering Panak or other male bears.

As she hurried along, she kept looking over her shoulder to see if they were being followed. When they came to snow too deep for the cubs to manage, she let them ride on her back. Even with the piggyback rides, the little bears soon grew tired trying to keep up with their mother. Despite their whines, Ursa continued on until she was confident they were out of danger.

Normally when the family rested, they simply stopped in their tracks. This time, however, Ursa led her cubs away from the shore and up a little slope. There was less chance of being ambushed here, and she could see over the bay. To conceal and shelter them she dug a shallow pit in the snow.

When she had finished scooping out the pit, she looked again to see if they were being followed. Nothing moved out on the ice, and there was no sign of Panak on their trail. After taking these precautions, Ursa nursed her cubs, sitting with her back against the wall of the pit. Tooga and Apoon were so tired that they fell asleep as soon as they'd been fed.

While the cubs slept in a heap on top of her, Ursa dozed with her head on the rim of the pit. Every few minutes she opened one eye to glance around. A few hours later, she roused the cubs and took them onto the ice-covered bay.

There was less snow on the bay than on the shore. In some places, the wind had blown the snow away entirely, leaving it as clean as a skating rink. In other spots where the snow had melted and then frozen, the ice was coated with a hard crust. The deepest snow and most of the drifts were on the lee side of the pressure ridges. These ridges were caused by the grinding action of the ice pans when they collided with each other.

Tooga and Apoon followed their mother onto the bay without difficulty. But when they stepped on the first icy patch, their feet went out from under them. It took them several tries to regain their feet, and more slipping and sliding before they learned to grip the ice with their little claws.

Visiting the bay was another new experience for the cubs. For their hungry mother, who had lost more than one third of her body weight, the bay was the key to her survival. During the winter she had lived off her fat reserve. Now that reserve was gone. Ursa knew that ringed seals lived beneath the wintry surface of the bay. Her challenge was to find them.

•

Ringed seals get their name from the pattern of pale circles on the sides of their gray coats. In the autumn they move from the open sea to the newly formed ice inshore. As the ice thickens, they keep at least two breathing holes open, and often use four or five breathing holes. Some of these holes are large enough for the seal to haul itself out onto the ice. By midwinter, most of the holes are hidden under the snow.

In late winter, ringed seal mothers dig out a birthing den over a snow-covered breathing hole. The cavern may be as long as a small car but is usually low and narrow. For this reason, snowdrifts on the lee side of pressure ridges are favorite den sites.

The pups are born with soft, crinkly white fur. For the first few weeks they are totally dependent upon their mother. The pups grow quickly and are weaned when they are a month old. At six weeks, their white coat has been replaced by a coat of silver gray with light circles, and they are on their own.

Ringed seals are a major food source for polar bears on the Labrador coast in the spring. In the struggle for survival, both animals have special talents. Polar bears have excellent noses and can smell a seal hidden under the snow the length of a soccer field away. Ringed seals, on the other hand, have sharp ears and can hear the crunch of a polar bear's footsteps on the ice from an amazing distance.

•

Ursa was familiar with the habits of ringed seals, and she had hunted them on the spring ice for several years. The most likely place to find them was in the drifts along the pressure ridges. The nearest pressure ridge was a long walk for the cubs, but they could rest along the way.

Soon after they set out, Ursa detected a thin thread of scent in the air. She stopped and studied the white landscape. From experience she knew the odor was filtering through the snow from a seal's breathing hole.

Leaving her cubs, she followed her nose. The smell led her toward a low snowdrift. As she drew closer, the smell became fainter. Sensing that something was wrong, Ursa rushed forward and pounced on the drift.

A few swipes of her paws uncovered the breathing hole in the ice. The seal had gone. Air bubbles were still coming to the surface, which meant she had missed the seal by seconds. Even though she had approached quietly, the seal must have heard her coming.

Ursa backed out of the drift and turned to rejoin her cubs. Instead of being where she left them, they were frolicking on a patch of snow behind her. From where she stood, she could hear the sound of their claws scraping on the crust.

The seal had heard it too.

Chapter Four

ON THE BAY

By the end of March the sun's rays had begun to soften the surface of the bay. Now, when the sun was out, the ice glistened with wet patches and puddles formed at the base of the melting drifts. Spring was just around the corner.

Tooga's mother had been hunting on the bay for nearly two weeks. Ringed seals were scarce and she had to cover a lot of ice searching for them. Of those she found, she had managed to catch four. These hard-earned meals were enough to keep her from starving, but did little to restore her weight. She was still painfully thin.

•

Ursa appeared to wander aimlessly over the frozen bay with her cubs, unaware of her surroundings. In fact, her nose was checking the breeze every step of the way, and she was constantly on the alert for seals.

In the first few days, the cubs often spoiled her hunting by not keeping still. After a week or so — and a few cuffs from their mother — Tooga and Apoon learned to keep quiet and absolutely still until the hunt was over.

Ursa also made the cubs swim soon after they stepped onto the bay. The icy seawater came as a shock to the little bears, but their natural walking movements kept them afloat. By watching their mother, they quickly learned to use their front paws to propel themselves, and to let their hind legs act as rudders.

When she was hunting, Ursa approached ridges or other promising places from the downwind side. Then, if a seal was hidden under the snow, its smell would be carried to her. This tactic increased her success, but often meant a long and tiring walk for the cubs.

Ursa always halted at the first whiff of a scent. Without moving, she would pinpoint the seal's lair and figure out the best way to approach it. After that she would place her cubs. If the seal was very close, she might lead the cubs away from it. Usually she left the cubs where they were.

•

It was now several days since Ursa had caught a seal. Just before dark she struck a scent that stopped her in mid-stride. The smell was coming from a snow-covered pressure ridge. It was so strong that she could detect two separate odors. One came from an adult seal, the other from a half-grown pup. The seals were together in a birthing den. Either seal would provide a huge meal.

The hungry bear began her stalk, placing each broad foot so that it didn't make a sound. At every step, the ribbon of scent connecting her to her quarry grew stronger. Silently she reached the edge of the drift.

The bear lowered her head and sniffed the snow to determine the exact location of the seals. Then, rearing up on her hind legs, she raised her massive forepaws and brought them crashing down on the spot.

Her paws sliced through the packed snow but glanced off the top of the den. Condensation from the seals' breath had formed a layer of ice on the ceiling. Normally Ursa could have punched through this ice barrier with a single blow. But she had lost so much weight that it took three tries to break into the den.

The first jarring crash woke the seals, who were sleeping on the ice near the entrance hole. The mother seal barked at her pup to flee, but the youngster was too stunned to move. At the next blow, the mother gave her pup a nip and pushed it into the water. Because the entrance hole was only big enough for one of them at a time, she had to wait for her pup to dive.

The bear's claws were coming through the roof as the mother seal slid into the water and made her escape.

•

That night Ursa decided to leave the bay. Ringed seals were increasingly hard to find, and their birthing season was almost over. If she stayed in the bay, her family could starve. It would be more dangerous for her cubs offshore, but there were many more seals, especially harp seals, on the pack ice.

•

Harp seals have gray fur with a band of darker fur across their body, which resembles a harp. The males have jet-black heads and rear flippers. Female harp seals are paler and sometimes have coin-sized spots instead of a horseshoe marking on their sides and back.

Harp seals move in herds with the arctic pack ice — following it north in the summer and south in the winter. From late February to early March thousands of harp seals have their pups off the coast of Labrador.

Harp seal mothers have a single baby, which is born on the open ice rather than in a sheltered den. Because the pups are covered with soft white fur, they are called "whitecoats" by commercial seal hunters.

The pups thrive on their mother's milk, which is ten times richer than cow's milk. When they are twelve to fourteen days old, they are abandoned by their mothers. By then the pups have tripled their weight and are as fat as stuffed sausages.

For the next six weeks they have nothing to eat, and they shed their white coats. While they are molting the young seals are known as "ragged jackets".

The pups lose half their body weight during this difficult period, but they emerge from it with sleek figures and coats of short, silver-gray fur. At this stage they become more active in the water and learn to feed themselves by catching fish.

•

Tooga and Apoon's muscles had grown stronger from all the walking they had done since leaving the den. Living outside had also thickened their coats and the fur on the soles of their feet, which gave them traction on the ice.

Even so, the trek to the pack ice was hard on the cubs. They had to walk against heavy winds all the way, and the surface underfoot became steadily rougher as they progressed. The only advantage of the wind was that it enabled their mother to smell what lay ahead — whether it was something to eat or something to fear.

On the third day they left the fast ice and crossed onto the pack ice. The pack ice was a mass of drifting ice floes. From the air, it resembled a floating jigsaw puzzle. The floes were forever changing shape, and the water-filled gaps between them were constantly opening and closing.

For the cubs' sake, Ursa avoided crossing wide stretches of open water. Tooga and his sister could swim, but at three-and-a-half months of age they couldn't stand the frigid water for more than a few minutes. When their mother crossed to another floe, she would choose the narrowest gap and swim with the cubs clinging to the fur on her back.

Once they reached the pack ice, Ursa kept a serious lookout for seals. This meant prowling the edges of the floes and the "leads", or cracks, in the pan ice. As well as hunting the edges, she also checked any breathing holes they encountered.

The cubs didn't hunt — nor would they for their first year — but they tried to copy their mother's every move. The young polar bears learned their survival skills through imitation. Thus, whenever Ursa broke into a ringed seal den on the bay, the cubs would totter about on their hind legs and whack the snow with their forepaws. On the pack ice, if she sniffed the edge of a floe to check if a seal had been there, the cubs would mimic her and sniff the same spot.

•

Whether they were hunting or traveling, the cubs stayed close to their mother. Sometimes they followed

her, one on each side. More often the family walked in a line, with Ursa in the lead, Apoon behind her and Tooga in the rear.

One morning, while they were picking their way through the pack ice, Ursa came upon a seal's breathing hole. The ice was so thick that the water in the hole was well below the surface. Ursa stopped briefly to investigate, then continued on. Apoon gave it a quick sniff and hurried to catch up with her mother, who was already out of sight.

Tooga walked slowly around the breathing hole. It was one of the largest he had seen — wide enough for two seals to get through at the same time. Curious to know more, he stood at the edge and peered into the opening. But the shadows made it hard for him to see the water.

Leaning as far forward as possible, the cub put his head down the seal hole. As he did so, his claws lost their grip on the slippery ice-covered rim.

Seconds later, he landed in the water with a splash.

CHAPTER FIVE

THE PACK ICE

Tooga got a bad fright when he fell into the breathing hole. Thrashing the water with his forepaws to stay afloat, he looked around the dark cavern. A bright circle of sky — the way out — was right above him. But every time he tried to reach it, his paws slipped on the glassy walls and he slid back down again.

With each attempt to escape he became weaker and more frightened. The icy water seemed to pull at him, and wouldn't let him go. He began to feel drowsy, and it was difficult to keep his head above water.

Tooga's head slipped under the surface for a few seconds, and he swallowed a mouthful of saltwater.

Meanwhile Tooga's mother — unaware of her cub's plight — continued on with Apoon trailing behind her. They had only gone a little way when she spied a young seal lying at the edge of a nearby floe. Before making her stalk, she turned to place the cubs and saw that Tooga was missing.

With a *Woof!* of alarm, Ursa bounded back down the trail, nearly knocking Apoon over as she rushed past. The mother bear had a strong suspicion of what had happened to her missing cub.

She made straight for the seal's breathing hole. When she got there, she had to lie on her stomach to see into the hole. It took a moment for her eyes to adjust to the dim light before she saw Tooga, floating limply in the water. Swiftly she reached down and scooped him out. He was unconscious but alive.

Ursa sat on the ice and held him close. While she warmed him with her body, she licked his fur to dry his sodden coat. Presently the little cub's eyes opened, and he snuggled deeper into his mother's fur. He was tired but he was safe.

It was an experience he would never forget.

After Tooga had rested and been fed, Ursa resumed her hunt. By then, the seal she had planned to catch was gone. An hour later, she was crossing a pressure ridge when she discovered a frozen baby harp seal lodged among the chunks of ice. The whitecoat had died in a storm when the floe it was on collided with another ice pan.

The mother bear ate the seal. It was her first meal in several days.

•

The main herd of harp seals had passed Saglek Bay on their way south more than a month before Ursa ventured onto the pack ice with her cubs. The herd was now far down the coast, but there were still some stragglers — both adults and young — in the area. As well as harp seals, there were also hooded seals, ringed seals, and a scattering of large bearded seals to be found on the floes.

It was difficult for the bear to approach adult seals on the open ice. Out of the water, the seals liked to stay near the edge of the floe or close to a breathing hole. Sometimes they lay so still they appeared to be asleep. But they were only dozing, and they would raise their heads frequently to look about. At the first hint of danger, they would slide back into the water.

Ursa found it frustrating to stalk these seals. Even

when she kept a low profile and moved slowly, they usually got away. Her challenge was to get close enough to her quarry — to do this she used another polar bear tactic. Instead of pursuing the seals, she let them come to her.

A few days later, while she was traveling with the cubs, she heard a seal bark, *Ark! Ark!* The sound came from the other side of a nearby ridge. Staying hidden, the mother bear peered through a gap in the ridge in the direction of the barks.

Try as she might, she couldn't find the seal. Finally she gave up the chance to surprise her victim, and stood on her hind legs for a better view. It was then she saw the breathing hole — just as a large harp seal disappeared below the water.

Ursa grunted at Tooga and Apoon to remain where they were, and silently padded over to the breathing hole. Then she lay down with her nose and forepaws close to the rim. While she waited for the seal, she didn't fidget or make a sound.

This type of "still hunting" was often unsuccessful. The seal might have three or four breathing holes and choose not to return to the one staked out by the bear. If the seal did return, there was a good chance it would see the bear. Whenever it saw the bear first, the seal was sure to escape.

Ursa had spent countless hours lying in wait at breathing holes. Her unblinking concentration on the water was one of the reasons for her success at still hunting. Even so, nine times out of ten she didn't make a kill. This time, however, she was lucky.

Less than half an hour later, a glossy black head popped out of the water. The instant the seal broke the surface, Ursa lunged forward and grabbed its head. As she crushed its skull with her teeth, she swept the flopping seal onto the ice with her paw. The ambush was over in seconds.

Still holding the dead seal by its head, the bear dragged it away from the hole. Tooga and Apoon, who had been watching their mother, bounded from their hiding place to join her. Ursa let the cubs sniff her trophy, then ripped a section of the seal's skin away with her teeth, and began to eat the blubber.

When she'd taken the edge off her hunger, she tore another strip of skin from the carcass for the cubs. Tooga and Apoon hadn't been weaned from their mother's milk and weren't much interested in solid food. They gave the blubber a few licks, then played tug-of-war with the strip of tough skin.

After Ursa had eaten her fill, she went back to the breathing hole. This time, she used the hole as a wash basin to clean the blood and grease from her chest, paws and muzzle. Having cleaned and groomed herself, she looked for a comfortable spot to feed her cubs.

She was lying on her side, nursing the cubs, when she noticed a flicker of movement among the floes. Her head went up and she stared at the spot. Everything appeared normal. A few minutes later, she saw something slip behind an upturned chunk of ice. Whatever it was, it was much closer.

Suddenly, Ursa was wide awake.

Tooga and Apoon felt their mother's body tense, and stopped feeding. Looking around, they were surprised to see a small white animal standing where they had played minutes before. The strange animal bent down, picked up their strip of sealskin, and boldly trotted off with it.

Ursa was relieved to see that the intruder was only a fox. She gave it a second look. There was something familiar about the animal. Then it came to her — it was the same fox that had traveled with her on the sea ice in the fall.

•

Kwa returned later that same day. This time he had his eye on the remains of the seal. Ursa showed her teeth and growled at him to keep his distance, even though he was not a threat to her cubs. Tooga and Apoon, who were standing behind their mother, also growled and showed their teeth at the little fox.

Kwa wasn't bothered by their hostility. He was used to bears growling at him. Several, including Panak, had even chased him. Being nimbler than his pursuers, it was easy for him to skip out of their way.

His chance came, as he knew it would, after the bear family bedded down for a rest. Once he was sure the mother bear was asleep, the fox stole quietly over to the seal carcass. When he had eaten, Kwa withdrew to his lair in the snowfield.

There, curled up with his nose in his bushy tail, he digested his meal.

Chapter Six

DANGER LOOMS

When Ursa woke, the afternoon sun was casting long blue shadows across the pack ice. She had slept heavily after feasting on the seal she caught that morning. The cubs were still asleep, draped across her back. The mother bear sniffed the wind, pushed the cubs aside, and stood up.

While she slept, a glaucous gull had discovered the dead seal. From the red-smudged footprints in the snow, Ursa could see that a fox had also been there. The fox was gone, but the large white gull was still picking at the remains. Neither the fox nor the gull had taken much from the carcass. There was still plenty of meat left for the bear to have another meal.

Ursa looked around, then rose on her hind legs to get a better view of the surrounding floes. At first glance, she saw nothing unusual across the barren expanse of ice and snow. She was about to turn away when she noticed a patch of yellow on a distant floe. She stared at the spot and saw that it was moving.

It was another polar bear.

The stranger disappeared behind a high ridge, then reappeared a minute or two later. The bear was directly downwind and heading toward her. Ursa assumed it was drawn by the smell of the dead seal. She could tell by the way it moved that it was an adult male. When the bear got closer, her worst fear was confirmed.

It was Panak.

There was no time to lose. She and the cubs must flee. Panak would probably stop to feed on the seal, which would give them a head start. But as soon as he was finished, he would come after them.

Tooga and Apoon didn't like being forced to walk so quickly. Nor did they understand why their mother was in such a hurry. She certainly wasn't hunting, for they had passed a number of breathing holes and she hadn't even given them a sniff.

The mother bear led the cubs in a wide arc, using the high drifts and snowy ridges to keep out of sight. In less than an hour they had circled behind Panak, and were now downwind of him. Their pursuer would have to trail them by foot scent, which would slow him down.

Ursa continued with the wind at her back until well after sunset. Then, under cover of darkness, she changed direction and turned north. Except for a few brief rest periods, the little family trudged all night. When the sun came up, there was no sign of Panak.

The mother bear had fooled him.

It was only then that Ursa stopped and allowed the cubs a long rest. By the end of the day Tooga and Apoon had recovered from their forced march, and their mother resumed hunting.

There was a fair number of seals in the area, including young ones that should have been easy to catch. During the next three days, however, the mother bear failed to make a kill. Bad luck was part of the reason for her lack of success.

•

By mid-April the melting ice was crisscrossed with water-filled channels that, from a distance, looked like pale blue veins. Ursa took advantage of these shallow channels to hide her approach when she was hunting seals in the open.

One morning, she made use of a channel to stalk a young hooded seal. It was a wonderful opportunity because the channel would allow the bear to approach within a single bound of her quarry.

Ursa grunted at Tooga and Apoon to lie down while she made her stalk. With her head resting on the water, she squeezed into the knee-deep channel and pushed off. She moved slowly and kept as low as possible.

At first the seal didn't notice her. But soon it became restless and began to stare in her direction. The seal's behavior puzzled the bear. She scrunched even lower.

Then, for no apparent reason, the seal slithered across the ice and dove into the water.

Ursa stood up and looked around.

Tooga had been following behind, faithfully imitating her movements. But instead of hiding in the channel, he had walked on the ice in full view of the seal. Ursa gave him a nip on the ear which brought a yelp from the little cub.

The next day — the fourth since the mother bear had eaten — she spotted another hooded seal on a nearby floe. The seal, which was lying at the very edge of the ice, also saw the bear. To escape, all the seal had to do was roll over and fall into the water.

Ursa watched the seal for some time before she came up with a plan. From experience she knew that a direct approach was certain to fail. Her only chance was to surprise the seal from another direction.

The bear crept along a channel that crossed the length of the floe. At the end of the channel she slipped into the water. With only her nose showing, she then turned and followed the edge of the ice back to the pan that held the seal. When she was close to the spot where the seal lay, she dove and swam underwater.

Ursa had placed the cubs so they could watch how she made the stalk. They were quite interested, as it was the first time they had seen their mother hunt this way. When she sank below the surface, they were mystified.

For about half a minute nothing happened. The seal continued to relax on the ice, while the bear simply disappeared.

Suddenly the water exploded at the edge of the floe, and the bear surged onto the ice. The seal was taken completely by surprise. Before it could escape, the bear seized it with her claws and crushed its head in her mouth, killing it instantly.

Tooga and Apoon, seeing that the hunt was over, ran across the ice to their mother. By the time they arrived, Ursa had already ripped open the seal and was gobbling the meat as fast as she could get it down. Hunger was not the only reason for her haste. She was afraid that a bigger bear might come along and take her meal.

Twenty minutes later, Panak appeared.

The mother bear was busy devouring the seal and didn't notice the huge intruder. It was only when Tooga growled that she looked up and saw Panak. She knew immediately why he had come. He had scented her kill and wanted it for himself.

If she didn't let him have the seal, he would take it by force. Panak was more than twice her size and, if it came to a fight, there was little chance she could defend her cubs or herself.

Keeping the cubs close, the mother bear backed away as Panak slowly lumbered toward her. When he

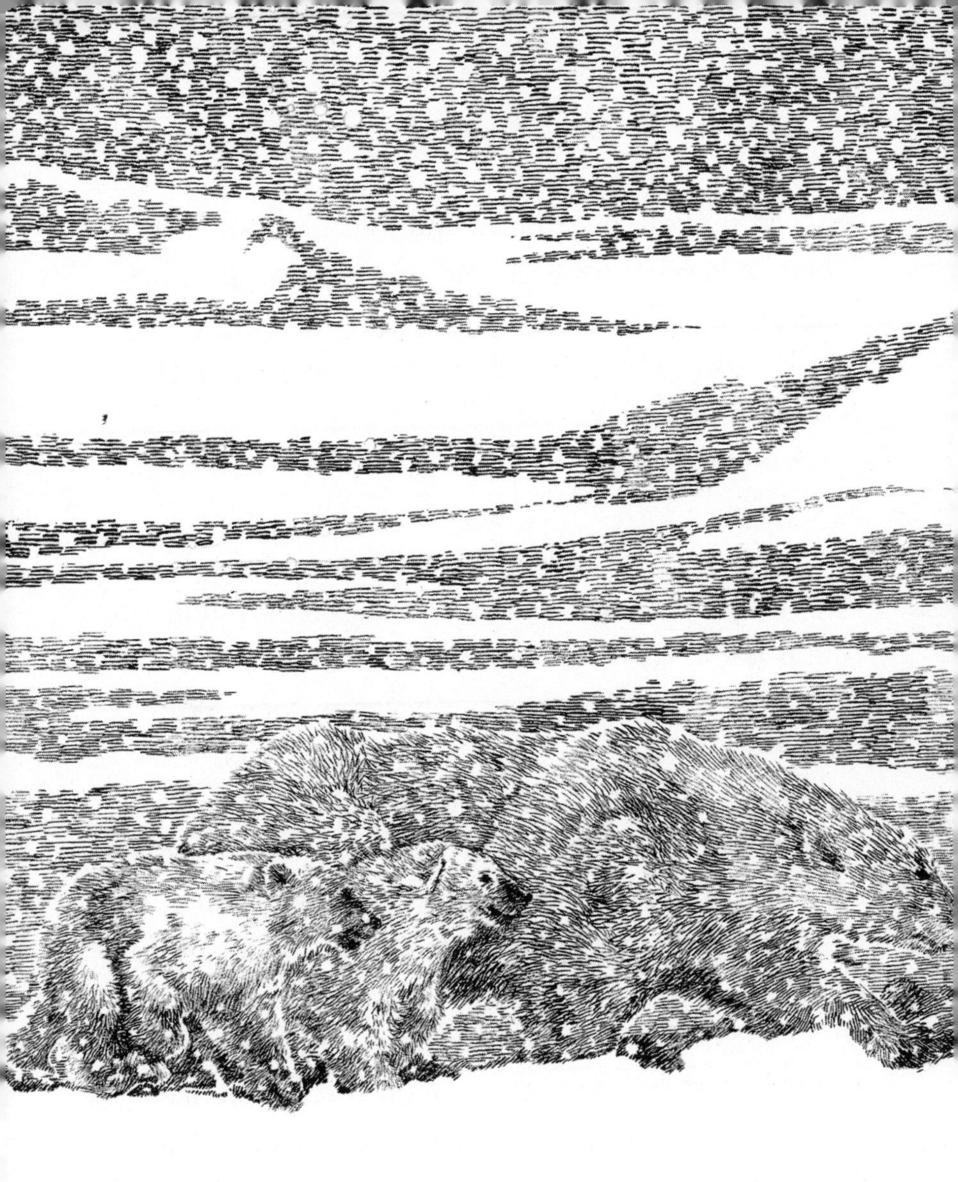

reached the seal, he stopped and looked down at it. Then he lowered his head and tore into the carcass. After his first bite, he didn't give the bear family another glance. For now, he was only interested in food.

While he was eating, Ursa quietly withdrew to a safe distance with her cubs. Then she led them through a gap in a nearby ridge. As soon as they were out of sight of Panak, she made Tooga and Apoon run as fast as their legs would carry them.

Shortly after they set off, it began to snow. From the fat wet flakes, and the wind direction, Ursa knew that a big storm was coming in from the ocean. Soon their coats were covered with snow and it was hard to see ahead. To make sure they were walking in the right direction, the mother bear kept the wind at her back.

The storm slowed the bear family's flight, but it also helped them to escape. Long before Panak had digested his stolen meal, the snow had covered their tracks — leaving no trace of where they had gone.

Chapter Seven

THE OUTERMOST ISLAND

By mid-June Ursa sensed it was time to leave the floes. The ice pans were breaking up, and those that were left were hardly thick enough to support her. No longer would a freezing night repair the melting of the previous day. Slowly but steadily the bear's feeding platform was shrinking and disappearing into the sea.

Closer to land the fast ice was gone, and a belt of open water now rimmed the coast. Having been through the sea-ice cycle before, this didn't surprise Ursa. Her only concern was for her cubs and how far they would have to swim to shore.

She knew the wind could help by pushing the pack ice closer to land. The prevailing wind was from the land to the sea. But at this time of year, it often blew onshore, bringing with it rain and fog. Rather than risk a long swim for the cubs, the mother bear decided she would wait and hope for a change in the wind.

•

On the eighteenth of June, the wind swung around from west to east. It blew fiercely for the next two days. Heavy seas broke up the floes, forcing the bears to scramble from one crumbling ice pan to another. Ursa wasn't worried the cubs would drown, but she feared that in the turmoil they might become separated from her.

Without their mother, the cubs would starve. At six months of age they still depended on her milk, and they were too young to hunt for themselves.

The gale pushed the pack ice tight to the shore in many places along the coast. The bear family's floe drifted against an island at the mouth of Saglek bay. There was no need for Tooga and Apoon to swim to safety. They simply stepped onto the ice-strewn beach.

The first thing their mother did after coming ashore was to investigate her new surroundings. For more than an hour she shambled about the island with the cubs, learning the lay of the land.

The island was the outermost of three low-lying islands. All three islands looked alike, with gravel beaches, low dunes and rock outcroppings. The vegetation was mainly sparse grass and clumps of stunted spruce trees. For a polar bear, there was little to eat on the islands.

The food shortage wouldn't be a serious problem for the bear family. Since Panak had forced Ursa to abandon her seal, the mother bear had enjoyed good hunting and put on a lot of weight. By late June she had enough fat on her to last until the autumn.

Although Tooga and Apoon had begun to eat solid food, their main nourishment still came from their mother, who nursed them every day.

•

The islands were snowbound for much of the year, but during the summer they came alive, attracting a host of birds. Some of the feathered visitors came from great distances to breed and raise their young. Despite the winter deep freeze, the combination of long sunlit days and intense heat also produced an amazing burst of plant and flower growth during the short northern summer.

It was often sweltering hot in July, even though there were still patches of snow on the hills, and icebergs of all shapes and sizes — some as tall as ten-story buildings — floated past the island every day like giant, white ice cubes.

•

The mother bear didn't enjoy summer on land. With her heavy coat, black skin, and thick layer of blubber, she suffered from the heat. On warm days she panted constantly, and it was an effort for her just to move around. She spent most of the summer trying to keep cool.

One way she lowered her body temperature was by lying on her back and spreading her limbs to take advantage of the breeze. She also rested in shallow daybeds. To insure she would be in the shade, she dug her beds on the north side of the dunes. Often she swam in the sea.

When she went to the water's edge, Ursa was careful to check if anything edible had come in with the tide. Usually there was nothing, and she had to settle for a clump of seaweed or a piece of kelp to chew on.

One day a walrus with long tusks washed up on the beach. The large seal-like animal had died of injuries in a fight with another walrus. Ursa had two big meals from the carcass before a high tide carried it away during a storm.

•

Tooga and Apoon had a wonderful summer. After their mother made sure there were no other bears on the island, she let the cubs roam about on their own. The heat didn't bother them, and they were full of energy.

The cubs spent a lot of time swimming in the ocean. This was quite natural, as polar bears are superbly adapted to the water, and even have a third eyelid that acts as a swim goggle when they submerge. Tooga and Apoon also wrestled and roughhoused with each other daily — both in and out of the water — and they played endless games of chase.

One of their favorite pastimes was to go exploring. Tooga, the bigger of the two cubs, led these expeditions. As the leader, he was the first to discover a family of Canada geese. He was also the first to be

chased away by the big old gander, which came at him with wings flapping, honking indignantly.

On another outing Tooga nearly stepped on an eider duck's nest in the gravelly stretch between the shore and the trees. At the last moment the mother duck flew off with a clatter, giving the cub a fright. He hadn't seen the eider duck on her down-lined nest because her brown and gray feathers blended perfectly with the surroundings.

By accident the cubs walked into the middle of a colony of Arctic terns on the dunes. The little white gulls — who had come all the way from South Africa for the summer — defended their chicks ferociously. With piercing shrieks they swirled over the two bears, diving at them from every direction. When one of the terns struck Tooga on the nose with its pointed red bill, he let out a squeak and fled.

A few days later, he almost stepped on a mother ptarmigan, another ground-nesting bird. Tooga didn't realize that the mottled brown bird that flushed was the same species as the white birds he had seen in the winter. Willow ptarmigan have white feathers in the winter to match the snow, and brown feathers in the summer to hide them on their nest.

The eider ducks and ptarmigan on the island needed this seasonal camouflage, as there were many gulls waiting to raid their nests. Given the chance, these winged predators would eat their eggs and swallow their chicks.

•

During the summer Ursa visited the other two islands on a regular basis, looking for food. The islands were only a short swim away, and she would take the cubs. These trips were fun for Tooga and Apoon but not very rewarding for their mother.

Ursa would usually catch a few lemmings and voles, although these rodents were so small it was hardly worth her effort to dig them out of their grass tunnels. After checking the beaches, she always returned to the outermost island.

Her food situation improved when the wild berries ripened in July. Ursa and the cubs swam from one island to the other to eat the blueberries, black crowberries, shiny red partridgeberries, and juicy yellow bake apples.

By mid-August most of the summer birds had gone. The goslings that the cubs had tried unsuccessfully to catch were now able to fly, and the goose family would soon be heading south. Summer was over.

Tooga and his sister had enjoyed a carefree time, with nothing to do but amuse themselves. Although they didn't know it, their play had strengthened their muscles and honed their survival skills — both of which they would need when they went back out on the sea ice in October.

They would spend most of the next year on the ice, returning to land only when the floes broke up. During the coming months, Tooga and Apoon would learn to hunt and to feed themselves.

Chapter Eight

ADRIFT

Tooga and Apoon were now two years old. It was the end of March, and once again they were on the pack ice with their mother. In the coming weeks Ursa would wean her cubs and the family would split up — a natural development in a polar bear family.

Already Ursa was less friendly toward her cubs, and she often pushed them away when they wanted to be fed. Not only was she reluctant to nurse them, but if they tried to join her when she was eating a seal, she wouldn't let them near it until she had finished her meal.

Tooga and Apoon's bonds with their mother were also loosening. Soon the cubs would go their separate ways. Last year, Tooga would rarely stray more than a stone's throw from his mother's side. Now he would spend most of his time on the pack ice out of her sight.

Although he was only two-thirds the size of his mother and not yet full grown, Tooga was becoming a good hunter. He was fortunate to have developed this skill as he was entering the most dangerous period in the life of a polar bear.

•

On the second of April a storm lashed the Labrador coast, causing the ice pans to heave and crash against each other. The day before the storm, Tooga had left his mother and sister and gone to the far edge of the pack ice to hunt seals. He sensed that a storm was coming before he set off, but he was used to bad weather and he ignored it.

Just before the storm, an eerie silence fell over the pack ice. The wind dropped and the sea turned calm. Minutes later the sky grew dark and the snow began to fall, whipped along by a powerful wind that tossed the waves and sent seawater sloshing across the ice pans.

Tooga retreated toward shore, the ice creaking and shaking beneath his feet at every step. After he'd gone a short distance, the ice felt firmer underfoot. He decided there was no need to go any farther. He would wait out the storm, as he had done many times before. Making himself comfortable, he curled up with his back to the wind, and fell asleep.

While the young bear slept, the waves continued to pound the pack ice. Bit by bit the outer edge began to crumble; and the steady battering sent shock waves under the ice pans, weakening their structures.

Tiny cracks suddenly expanded into wide channels, and the sheets of ice began to shift and grind against each other. At the height of the storm, a deep crack appeared at the edge of the main floe. The crack curved inland, tracing a jagged path down the coast before returning to the sea far below where it had begun.

When the storm ended and the wind shifted around to the northwest, this long crack opened up like a giant zipper. A huge section of the floe — large enough to encompass a small town — split from the main ice pack and slowly floated out to sea.

•

Tooga slept through the storm. When he woke, he had no idea that anything was wrong. Although he was on the piece that had broken away, it was so vast that everything looked normal to him. Nor did he sense any unusual motion. He was used to the movement of the pack ice, and this floe seemed no different than others he had been on.

After he'd stretched and sniffed the wind, he went hunting as usual. Because seals like to congregate at the edge of the ice, there was a good number of them — ringed, harp and hooded seals — riding the floe with him.

In the next few hours he saw five different seals, but all of them submerged before he could stalk them. Later, as he rounded an iceberg in the floe, he came upon an adult harp seal. It was basking on a sheet of ice, close to the water. The seal was shedding its winter coat, and its fur was in patches.

Tooga knew that molting seals, because of their skimpy coats, didn't like to go into the cold water unless it was necessary. Usually they would wait until the last moment before making their escape. This hesitation made them easier to catch and was often their undoing.

Tooga stalked the harp seal carefully and was able to get close enough to make his final charge. Pouncing on the seal, he grabbed it with both forepaws. The seal squirmed violently and slipped from his grip into the water, leaving the young bear with two paws full of loose seal fur.

After this failure Tooga decided to rejoin his mother, hoping that she would feed him. Turning his back to the sea, he walked inland to find her. An hour later he found himself at the edge of the floe again, looking at the sea.

This was puzzling!

He made three more attempts to go inland before he gave up. He would look for his mother another day. Meanwhile he would have to catch a seal to feed himself.

•

Tooga never did find his mother. It wasn't a serious setback for him, as he was ready to be weaned and he no longer needed his mother's milk. His diet was mainly seal meat, and there were enough seals on the floe to keep him well fed.

As the weeks went by, he gradually forgot about his family.

•

By June the floe had shrunk dramatically and the ice was getting soft. Each day it was becoming more difficult for Tooga to find ice pans that would support him. Soon the floe would break up, and he would have to swim to shore.

As the floe was carried south by the Labrador Current, the wind brought him more and more unfamiliar odors from the settlements along the coast. The young bear knew nothing about humans, but the smells disturbed him. He sensed they foretold danger.

On the twenty-third of June, the wind changed from west to east. For the next three days the flow of warm air over the ice shrouded the Labrador coast in fog. The onshore wind pushed the floe that Tooga was riding into Sandwich Bay.

The sight of land prompted the young bear to leave the floe and swim for the nearest shore.

He emerged from the water at the edge of a settlement on the bay. After shaking himself, he stood for a long while trying to get his bearings. He couldn't decide what direction he should take. The scent of something to eat made up his mind. Following the scent through the fog, he headed inland.

The smell drew him on, but with each step he became more nervous. A house loomed out of the fog. The smell of frying fish wafted from a window on the ground floor of the house. The bear paused at the edge of the rutted driveway, unsure what to do next.

While he was standing by the gravel drive, he heard an unfamiliar squeaking sound. The sound was coming toward him. Seconds later, a little girl on a bicycle nearly ran into him.

The bear and the girl stopped and stared at each other.

•

At supper that evening, the girl's older brother teased her for making up stories.

"Who's going to believe you saw a polar bear by the back door? Are you sure it wasn't an elephant?"

"It's true! I did! And the bear looked at me, and I looked at him, and then he just sort of walked away. . . ."

The girl's mother intervened. "Well, dear, in this fog it's easy to think you've seen something. When I was your age I used to imagine I'd seen all sorts of things."

"But I did, I saw a white bear! Honest, I really did!"

"OK, I'll tell you what we'll do," said her father. "After supper we'll go outside and look for the bear's tracks."

The family searched up and down the drive, and the bit of grass on both sides, without seeing any sign of the bear. They were about to go in when the little girl called to her father.

"Dad, what's this mark in the mud?"

Her father looked down at the broad five-toed print at the edge of the puddle. Then he put his hand over the print, and spread his fingers wide to measure it.

"Honey, that's your bear."

Chapter Nine

SANDWICH BAY

The girl on the bicycle hadn't frightened Tooga. But the noises coming from the house — the rattle of dishes, radio music, and the sound of a slamming door — made him uneasy. He didn't understand what caused these sounds, and he thought he'd better leave.

When he disappeared into the fog, the little girl couldn't see which way he had gone. Instinctively Tooga headed inland along the north shore of Sandwich Bay. The next morning he reached the mouth of the White Bear River and swam across the river to Separation Point.

This thin spit of land separated the White Bear from the Eagle River. The two rivers were so close together that a person could stand on the bank of one river and throw a stone over Separation Point into the other river.

After shaking the water from his coat, the young bear wandered about on Separation Point for some time, unable to decide which river to follow. Eventually he continued inland along the bank of the Eagle River.

The Eagle River was so wide at Separation Point that it formed part of the tidal water of the bay. As Tooga padded upstream, the river became narrower and swifter. It was dark by the time he reached the gorge, where the river rushed through a high rock canyon.

The walls of the gorge came straight down to the water, leaving no room for him to walk along the shore, and the walls were too steep for the bear to climb. When he tried to swim against the thundering torrent, Tooga was instantly swept downstream.

After several attempts to fight the current, he realized — as his ancestors had known — that the best way around this obstacle was to leave the river and walk through the forest over the hill.

A few minutes later Tooga emerged from the trees and found himself on a stone ledge at the head of the gorge. Before him lay a round pool the size of a small lake. At the far end of the pool, the river narrowed again into a series of low falls and rapids.

From where he stood, Tooga had a good view of the pool in the moonlight. A single salmon leapt into the air and fell back with a splash. Presently another salmon jumped at the base of the falls. Tooga was about to move up to the falls when he was stopped by a delicious smell coming from somewhere downstream.

The smell was so enticing that he retraced his steps and went back down the hill to the foot of the gorge. As he walked down the river, the smell grew stronger. A short distance below the gorge, he came to a small dock with two boats moored to it.

Just below the dock Tooga lost the scent. To recapture the scent, he walked back and forth along the bank, sniffing the wind. Soon he picked up the trail again.

It led him to a fishing camp at the edge of the forest. No light showed in the low wooden building. As he got closer, he was able to pinpoint the source of the delicious odor. It was coming from the screened porch.

Tooga pressed his nose against the screen and peered inside. Then, as though swatting a fly, he ripped a hole in the screen and shambled through the opening to the barbecue. On the way, he knocked over several folding metal lawn chairs.

"Pipe down out there! People are trying to sleep!"

Intent on the barbecue, the bear ignored the muffled voice. The smell of grease and spicy sauce made him drool. Picking up the barbecue, he tried to get at the grill but couldn't open the metal cover. After wrestling with it briefly, he hurled the barbecue against the wall of the cabin.

"Hey, you on the porch, get to bed — it's after midnight!"

The young bear paused for a moment at the sound of the angry voice before picking up the barbecue and flinging it on the floor with a crash.

Inside the cabin there were furious rumblings and the thud of bare feet.

Taking notice of the commotion, Tooga rose on his hind legs and stood at the door to listen.

Suddenly a man with a flashlight opened the door.

The man was muttering to himself, "Some people are so selfish they don't care about — " when the beam of his flashlight shone on the white bear standing in the doorway. The man stopped in mid-sentence. After a shocked silence, he slammed the door in the bear's face.

Tooga wasn't disturbed by the intrusion nor by the frantic whispering and patter of feet inside the cabin. As soon as the door closed, he dropped onto all four paws and resumed his search for something to eat.

Luckily for him, when the barbecue hit the floor, it bounced against a large cooler chest. The force knocked the lid of the chest open to reveal the camp's perishable food — eight large steaks, a cooked ham, some packages of bacon, several dozen eggs, a tub of butter, and a frozen chicken.

Tooga started by eating the steaks and the paper they were wrapped in. Then he gobbled down the bacon and the ham in their sealed plastic packages. The butter, which reminded him of blubber, was a particular treat. The eggs were messy.

The fishermen watched through the windows of the cabin while the polar bear demolished their supply of fresh meat. One of the men suggested they make loud noises to scare the bear away. Nobody had a gun, so they began banging the kitchen pots and pans together.

At first Tooga was too busy eating to notice the din. But after he'd consumed almost everything in the cooler chest, the racket began to get on his nerves. It was time to go. He left through the hole he had torn in the screen, taking the frozen chicken with him.

At the riverbank he paused to consider which direction he should take. He could go downstream to Sandwich Bay or upstream to the big pool with the falls. His instinct told him to go downstream. At first light he left the river and went into the deep woods to digest his meal.

That afternoon he resumed his journey and arrived at Separation Point just before midnight. Instead of crossing the White Bear River, he swam to the other side of the Eagle River and walked along the opposite shore toward the coast. Because of the heat, he took frequent swims to cool off along the way.

The next morning the pilot of a commercial float plane spotted the bear as he was coming out of the water near the entrance to Sandwich Bay. The pilot radioed his sighting to the provincial wildlife officer in the nearby settlement of Cartwright.

•

Two days later, the wildlife officer in Cartwright received another call about Tooga. This time it was from a crab-processing plant. A polar bear had been seen loitering downwind of the plant. Like the local black bears, the polar bear was undoubtedly drawn by the smell of the cooking snow crabs.

The call ended with, "The bear's getting closer, and it seems to be getting bolder. If you don't deal with it soon, somebody could get hurt!"

After the man from the crab plant hung up, the wildlife officer quickly phoned half a dozen members of the Canadian Rangers, the northern militia. The message was the same to each person — telling him that there was a polar bear at the crab plant, where to meet, and not to forget his rifle.

CHAPTER TEN

THE TREK NORTH

Tooga spun around at the loud *Crack!* of a rifle. The shot was fired by a man standing behind the polar bear in a clearing among the trees. A moment later a barrage of rifle shots echoed through the forest, and more men in red jackets appeared on both sides of the first man.

The noise of the shots startled Tooga and hurt his ears. As the men advanced toward him, the rattle of gunfire grew louder. He forgot about the delicious smell coming from the crab plant. His only wish was to escape from the men and the terrible noise they made.

Looking about for an escape route, he saw red jackets closing in on three sides — from the east, west, and south. The only way out was to the north.

He set off at a trot with his pursuers at his heels.

The men followed Tooga for more than an hour. He thought he had left the men behind when he took to the water and swam across the bay. Yet, when he waded ashore and looked over his shoulder, two of the men were watching him from a boat.

Tooga didn't know that the wildlife officer and the Rangers had herded him away from the fish plant for his own safety, and they had taken care to drive him north toward his homeland.

On the other side of the bay, the young bear retreated into the spruce forest and wandered aimlessly for several days. Hunger drew him back to the seacoast in search of food. The next day he found the rotting carcass of a seal in a little cove, and ate most of the remains.

He was lying in the shade, trying to keep cool, when he was seized by an urge to return to the place where he was born. To get there, his instinct told him he must continue north. As there was no path to take, he would have to follow the ragged coastline.

Fortunately Tooga was in good physical condition, having eaten well on the floes while he was drifting south. And though a young and inexperienced bear, he now knew enough to avoid humans. That same day, he started the long trek home.

•

Viewed from the sea, the close-packed spires of the dark spruce trees gave the coastline a jagged silhouette. In many places, slabs of smooth gray rock sloped to the water's edge, while in some of the coves there were gravel beaches.

Onshore the bushes and trees were stunted, and the underlying rock lay close to the surface. Lichen-covered rock outcroppings were everywhere, interspersed with patches of ivory-colored moss and trailing groundcover with shiny green leaves. Despite the harsh climate and the shallow soil, there were many wildflowers.

•

Whenever possible, Tooga swam across the bays and inlets rather than walk around them. He also used the islands that dotted the coast as stepping stones — especially when faced with a long swim. In the same way, when he came to a point of land or a peninsula and he could smell water on the other side of it, he would cut across the base rather than go around it.

Although he was constantly hungry, the first six

weeks of his journey went smoothly. Whenever he neared a settlement, he hid in the forest during the day and traveled after dark to avoid being seen. By taking this precaution, he was able to swim across the inlet between Makkovik and Aillick without being detected.

His luck changed a few weeks later, when he was crossing from one island to another.

By accident, he swam into a fisherman's net. The gill net was underwater, suspended from the surface by cork floats — like a long blanket hanging from a clothesline. It was designed so that, when a fish bumped into it, the fish's head would go through one of the mesh openings. When the fish tried to back out, the gill covers on either side of its head would catch on the mesh and it couldn't escape.

Tooga could have backed away after bumping into the net — his head was much too big to go through it — but he noticed a salmon below him caught in the mesh. When he dove down to grab the salmon, he became caught in the folds of the net. The cord was too strong for him to break. The more he thrashed about the more deeply he became entangled.

•

Early the next morning, an old man in a wooden dory rowed out to check his net. When he got close to the net, he looked over his shoulder and saw something white splashing on the surface. The man's eyesight was poor and, assuming it was a salmon, he rowed over to pick it up.

At the last moment a warning growl alerted the old fisherman to his mistake. The man jumped with fright and grabbed a boathook in the bottom of his boat. Without thinking, he swung the long wooden pole and struck the bear a glancing blow on the head. The metal hook pierced one of the bear's small round ears.

Enraged by the pain, Tooga broke free and surged out of the water. Had he not been held by the last two unbroken strands, he would have climbed into the boat. After fumbling frantically with his oars, the man rowed away, slapping the surface in his haste to escape. The bear watched the boat until it disappeared from view behind an island.

By then Tooga was free of the net and swimming as fast as he could toward another island. He hid on the island until dark, then continued north that night.

•

The long trek north took a toll on the young bear. After leaving Sandwich Bay in July, he had little to eat except scraps of carrion, small rodents, seaweed, and wild berries. By the end of August, he had lost all the fat he had accumulated in the spring, and his strength was failing. Because of his weakened condition he had to rest more often, and for longer periods.

The exhausted bear was resting in the crater of an uprooted tree near Davis Inlet when he smelled the odor of a rotting whale. Tooga's sensitive nose told him the dead whale was some distance away — at least a day's walk up the coast. Summoning the last of his strength, he went to look for it.

The whale wasn't hard to find. As Tooga got closer, the smell became almost overpowering, and a cloud of seagulls wheeled in the sky above the spot where it lay. The whale was black and nearly as long as a school bus. It had died from a collision with a commercial fishing vessel.

The gulls were the only scavengers feeding on the whale, and the bear had no difficulty shouldering them aside for a place to eat. After so long without a good meal, he gorged himself until he could barely walk.

He stayed in the area and fed heavily on the carcass for more than a week. During this time he put on weight and regained a lot of his strength.

•

In early September, when the first snow flurries began, Tooga resumed his journey.

The cooler weather made it easier for him to travel, and he was able to cover more ground every day. Each morning the freezing overnight temperatures left a layer of ice on the ponds, and vapor rose like smoke from the sheltered bays. At night, the sky glowed and shimmered with undulating waves of color from the northern lights.

As he continued north, the terrain grew increasingly familiar. This lifted his spirits and told him he was nearing home.

•

In mid-October, when the fast ice along the shoreline became thick enough to support his weight, Tooga responded to an age-old instinct. Changing direction, he left the coast and headed out onto the sea ice to hunt seals. It took him three days, and many hours of waiting motionless at breathing holes, before he caught his first seal.

Lest a bigger bear take his meal, he wasted no time in eating it. After the first frantic minutes gobbling down the blubber, he looked around to see if another bear had scented his kill.

To his relief, the only predator in sight was an arctic fox. As Tooga turned away, it struck him that he had seen the little animal somewhere before. When the white fox stepped closer, the bear got a good look at him. It was Kwa.

Tooga was home at last.

AUTHOR'S NOTE

Tooga's story is fiction, but it is based on fact.

In the normal course of events, after Ursa and her cubs separated, they would not meet again. Ursa would probably mate the following spring and have another litter of cubs. Apoon, if she survived the first difficult year on her own, would mate and have cubs when she was about five years old.

Tooga would eventually grow to be twice the size of his mother and his sister, but would not mate until he was six or seven years old.

Like Tooga, each spring a few polar bears are caught on the ice floes and carried south by the Labrador Current. Some have traveled more than 1000 kilometers (600 miles). Sandwich Bay, where Tooga came ashore, is still visited by an occasional stray polar bear.

The settlement of Cartwright was named for an English adventurer, Captain George Cartwright (1739–1819), who spent sixteen years on the coast of Labrador. Cartwright named the Eagle and White Bear Rivers in 1775, noting in his journal that both rivers "were much frequented by salmon and bears."

On July 22, 1778, George Cartwright stood on the ledge above the gorge on the Eagle River and counted 33 white bears and 3 black bears feeding on salmon at the base of the rapids.

Today — because of the advance of civilization, global warming, and other human factors — polar bears are rarely seen on the Eagle River.

GLOSSARY

ambush — a surprise attack from a hiding place
Apoon — a name derived from an Inuit word for "snow"
arctic fox — a northern fox whose fur is gray-brown in summer and white in winter
arctic tern — a small seabird that breeds in the arctic and winters in the Antarctic
arctic willow — a low willow bush that grows in northern Canada
bake apple — the fruit of the cloudberry plant, a Newfoundland delicacy
Beluga — a small white whale that is found off the Labrador coast
birthing den — a place where the mother gives birth to her babies; see natal den
blizzard — a heavy snowstorm with intense cold and high winds
blubber — a thick layer of fat under the skin of seals and other animals
Canada goose — wild goose with a black neck, gray wings and white and gray body
Canadian Rangers — a volunteer force that provides military presence in remote areas
carrion — the rotting flesh of a dead animal
Cartwright, Capt. George — author of a three-volume Labrador journal from 1770 to 1786
Cartwright — a settlement at the mouth of Sandwich Bay named for Captain George Cartwright
crowberry — a low evergreen shrub with purple flowers and black berries

dory — a small flat-bottomed boat with a high bow and stern
Eagle River — a renowned Atlantic salmon river that empties into Sandwich Bay
Eider duck — a large sea duck; the female lines her nest with down from her body
fast ice — ice that forms from the land in the fall, and melts in the summer
foot scent — the odor left on the ground by the feet of an animal
gill net — a net suspended in the water to catch fish by their gills in the mesh
Glaucous gull — a large white seagull found in northern regions
guard hairs — the coarse hairs that form a protective coat over underfur
Gyrfalcon — a rare northern falcon with three color phases: white, gray, and dark gray
hackles — the hair on the back of the neck of an animal that rises when it is angry or afraid
hibernation — to sleep (usually in a den) through the winter
ice floe — a large expanse of sea ice
Inuit — the native people of northern Canada and the surrounding polar regions
kelp — a long ribbonlike type of seaweed
Kwa — name derived from an Inuit word for "frozen"
Labrador — the coastal region of northeastern Canada, part of Newfoundland
Labrador Current — a cold ocean current that flows south, often causing fog

lead — an opening or space between ice pans
lee — the sheltered side, or the side away from the wind
lemming — a small rodent, similar to a vole, that lives in the arctic and subarctic
lichen — a crusty fungus that grows in patches on rocks and trees, etc.
lowlands — the flat or marshy areas that are below the surrounding terrain
militia — part-time soldiers who perform military service in emergencies
molt — to shed fur (or feathers) while undergoing a change of coat
natal den — see birthing den
northern lights — common name for the night-sky display of the aurora borealis
offshore wind — a wind that blows from the land out to sea
onshore wind — a wind that blows from the sea onto the land
pack ice — a large mass formed from pieces of floating ice
Panak — name derived from an Inuit word for "snow knife"
pan ice — sheets or flat sections of floating ice
partridgeberry — a creeping plant with white flowers and scarlet berries
predator — an animal that eats other animals; also called a carnivore
pressure ridge — a ridge on the pack ice caused by the grinding action of ice pans
prey — an animal that is hunted by another animal for food
ptarmigan — a northern grouse that has white plumage in winter

quarry — an animal that is hunted by other animals
raven — a large bird similar to a crow with black feathers and a hoarse croak
Saglek Bay — a large bay on the northern coast of Labrador
Sandwich Bay — a large bay on the southern coast of Labrador
scavenger — an animal that eats dead animals killed by others
sea ice — any floating ice on the sea, but usually refers to the offshore pack ice
Separation Point — a narrow spit of land between the Eagle and White Bear rivers
snowdrift — a pile-up of snow, usually caused by the wind
snow ridge — a ridge of snow shaped by the wind
spruce tree — an evergreen tree with a narrow shape and short needles
Tooga — name derived from an Inuit word for "ivory"
tundra — flat, treeless country in the arctic and subarctic
underfur — short dense fur next to an animal's skin
Ursa — name derived from the Latin word for "bear"
vole — a small rodent, similar to a mouse with a short tail
White Bear River — a short river that empties into Sandwich Bay
whitecoat — a baby harp seal with white fur, usually less than three weeks old